TIMELESS CLASSICS

THE ADVENTURES OF
TOM SAWYER
Mark Twain

– ADAPTED BY –
Joanne Suter

SADDLEBACK
EDUCATIONAL PUBLISHING

TIMELESS CLASSICS

Literature Set 1 (1719-1844)
A Christmas Carol
The Count of Monte Cristo
Frankenstein
Gulliver's Travels
The Hunchback of Notre Dame
The Last of the Mohicans
Oliver Twist
Pride and Prejudice
Robinson Crusoe
The Swiss Family Robinson
The Three Musketeers

Literature Set 2 (1845-1884)
The Adventures of Huckleberry Finn
The Adventures of Tom Sawyer
Around the World in 80 Days
Great Expectations
Jane Eyre
The Man in the Iron Mask
Moby Dick
The Prince and the Pauper
The Scarlet Letter
A Tale of Two Cities
20,000 Leagues Under the Sea

Literature Set 3 (1886-1908)
The Call of the Wild
Captains Courageous
Dracula
Dr. Jekyll and Mr. Hyde
The Hound of the Baskervilles
The Jungle Book
Kidnapped
The Red Badge of Courage
The Time Machine
Treasure Island
The War of the Worlds
White Fang

SADDLEBACK
EDUCATIONAL PUBLISHING
www.sdlback.com

Copyright © 1999, 2011 by Saddleback Educational Publishing
All rights reserved. No part of this book may be reproduced or transmitted in any form or by any means, electronic or mechanical, including photocopying, recording, or by any information storage and retrieval system, without the written permission of the publisher. SADDLEBACK EDUCATIONAL PUBLISHING and any associated logos are trademarks and/or registered trademarks of Saddleback Educational Publishing.

ISBN: 978-1-61651-069-5
eBook: 978-1-60291-803-0

Printed in the United States
26 25 24 23 22   7 8 9 10 11

TIMELESS CLASSICS

Contents

	Foreword 4
1	The Glorious Whitewasher 5
2	War, Love, and Sunday School 12
3	Heartbreak 19
4	Murder in the Graveyard 25
5	The Pirate Crew Sets Sail 32
6	Pirates at Their Own Funeral 40
7	Tom Takes Becky's Punishment 45
8	Saving Muff Potter 50
9	The Buried Treasure 56
10	Tom and Becky in the Cave 63
11	Floods of Gold 71
	Afterword 79
	Activities 80

Foreword

Some of the adventures in this book happened to me and some happened to friends of mine. Huck Finn and Tom Sawyer are based on boys I knew. My book is meant to entertain boys and girls. But I hope it will also be read by men and women. I hope it reminds adults of how they once thought and talked and of the strange things they did.

—The Author

1

The Glorious Whitewasher

"Tom!"

No answer.

"Tom! Where is that boy? You, TOM!"

The old lady looked over the top of her glasses. "If I lay hold of you, I'll..."

She did not finish her threat but looked under the bed. There was no boy there. She went to the front door and shouted again, "Y-o-uu *Tom!*"

A noise came from behind her. Turning quickly, she grabbed a small boy by the shirt.

"There you are, you rascal! What have you been doing?"

"Nothing."

"Nothing? Why, look at your sticky hands. And look at your mouth! How many times have

I told you to leave that jam alone? Hand me that switch."

The switch was raised in the air.

"My! Look behind you, Aunt!"

The old lady whirled around.

The boy ran out the door. In an instant, he had scrambled over the fence and disappeared.

His Aunt Polly stared at the empty room. Then she broke into a gentle laugh. "Will I never learn?" she said to herself. "Hasn't Tom Sawyer played tricks enough on me? But they say old fools is the biggest fools! And that boy never plays the same trick twice. I'm afraid I've spoiled him. But he's my own dead sister's boy, poor thing. I just ain't got the heart to lash him!"

Aunt Polly sighed. "Chances are he'll skip school this afternoon," she thought. "Then I'll have to make him work on Saturday. He hates work more than he hates anything else, but I've got to do my duty."

Aunt Polly was right. Tom *did* play hooky, and he had a very good day.

He got home in time to sit down at the supper table with his younger brother, Sid. Sid was a quiet boy. He never went out on adventures and never made any trouble.

While Tom was eating supper—and stealing sugar when he could—Aunt Polly asked questions. It was clear she wanted to trap him into admitting he'd played hooky.

"My, it was warm today, wasn't it, Tom? Didn't you want to go a-swimming?"

"No ma'am. Not very much."

The old lady reached out and felt Tom's shirt. She found it was dry.

Tom knew what was coming next. "Some of us pumped water on our heads," he said. "See, my hair is still damp."

Aunt Polly thought a moment. "When I sewed that rip in your shirt this morning, Tom, I also stitched your collar shut. Open your jacket!"

Tom opened his jacket.

"Well, I'll be! I was *sure* you'd been a-swimming. But look at your collar still sewed tight." Aunt Polly felt proud. For once she thought Tom had done the right thing.

But then Sid spoke up. "Well now, I thought you sewed his collar with white thread. But look, that thread is black."

"Why, I *did* sew it with white! TOM!"

But Tom was out the door. "Sid," he shouted back, "I'll lick you for that!"

It was true that Tom was not the model boy of the village. He knew the model boy very well—and hated him.

Saturday morning came bright and fresh and full of life. The trees were in bloom and there was a song in every heart.

Tom appeared on the sidewalk with a bucket of whitewash and a brush. He looked at the fence mournfully. All gladness was gone. The time had come to take his punishment for skipping school.

There were more than 30 yards of fence to whitewash! Sighing, Tom dipped his brush in the bucket. Then he sighed again and sat down on a wooden box. Pretty soon his friends would come along. They would make fun of him for having to work. Just the thought of it burnt him like fire.

He reached in his pocket and got out all his worldly goods. There were bits of toys, marbles, and trash—not half enough to buy his freedom. Then an idea came to him—a *wonderful* idea! He took up his brush and went happily to work.

Before long, Ben Rogers came along. Ben was hopping and skipping, proof that his heart was light. He was eating an apple and making deep-toned ding-dong sounds like a steamboat.

Tom went on whitewashing. He paid no attention to the steamboat sounds.

"Hello, old chap," called Ben. "You got to work, hey?"

Tom looked around. "Why, Ben! I didn't notice you."

"Say, Tom, I'm going a-swimming today," bragged Ben. "Don't you wish you could? But of course, you got to *work!*"

"What do you call work?" asked Tom.

"Why, ain't that work?"

Tom kept whitewashing. "Well, maybe it is, and maybe it ain't. All I know is, a boy doesn't get a chance to whitewash a big fence like this every day."

That put things in a new light. Ben watched Tom carefully sweeping his brush back and forth.

Tom stepped back and looked at his work. He added a touch here. Then he added a touch there. He looked proud and pleased.

Ben watched. "Say, Tom," he said, "let me whitewash a little."

Tom thought a minute. "No—no, I can't do that. Aunt Polly says this work is too important. I reckon there ain't one boy in a thousand that can paint it right."

"I'll be careful," promised Ben. "Say—I'll give you my apple if you let me!"

Tom slowly gave up his brush. He looked

unwilling, but inside his heart was dancing. While Ben worked and sweated in the sun, Tom sat munching the apple.

There was no lack of painters who fell for Tom's trick. Boys came to tease, but stayed to whitewash. Tom traded chances to paint the fence for a kite, a dead rat, 12 marbles, and a piece of blue glass. He also got a key that wouldn't unlock anything, a couple of fine tadpoles, a brass knob, and a dog collar—but no dog.

All morning Tom had plenty of company, and the fence got three coats of whitewash!

Tom had discovered something important about human nature. He learned that people will always want *anything* that is hard to get! Indeed, the writer of this book knows that *work* is something that a person *has* to do, while *play* is whatever a person does *not* have to do.

For a while Tom thought about what he had learned. Then he skipped into the house to report to Aunt Polly.

| 2 |
War, Love, and Sunday School

"My stars!" cried Aunt Polly. "Why, I can't believe it!" She stared at the fence. "You can work when you want to, Tom Sawyer!" She took Tom into the house and gave him an apple. On the way outdoors, he grabbed a doughnut, too.

As he skipped off to play, Tom saw Sid. There were dirt clods handy, and the air was soon full of them. They fell on Sid like a hailstorm. Then Tom was over the fence and gone. He was at peace now that he'd settled things with Sid for getting him in trouble.

Tom hurried to the muddy alley behind the cow barn. He had to meet Joe Harper there for an important army battle. Tom was general of one of the armies. Joe was general of the other. That day, Tom's army won the hard-fought fight.

The dead were counted. The prisoners were exchanged. Then both armies marched away. Tom turned toward home, alone.

As he passed Jeff Thatcher's house, Tom saw a new girl in the garden. The lovely, blue-eyed creature wore a white summer dress. She had two long, yellow braids. All thoughts of his old love, Amy Lawrence, had suddenly disappeared. Now Tom worshipped this new angel. He began to show off. He jumped about and did handstands—anything to get her attention.

But the girl said nothing. She moved toward the house, leaving Tom hanging on the fence, lovesick. Then, just before going inside, the girl paused. She tossed a flower over the fence—right to Tom!

Tom picked up the flower. He tucked it inside his jacket, next to his heart—or his stomach, maybe. (He wasn't too sure where those parts were.) Then he showed off some more, hoping the girl was watching from a window. But he didn't see her again that day.

At supper Tom's spirits were high. His aunt wondered what had got into the child.

When Aunt Polly left the room, Sid knocked over the sugar bowl. The model child is going to catch it now, Tom grinned. But before Tom knew it, Aunt Polly was raising her hand to *him!*

"Hold on! What are you belting me for?" Tom cried. "*Sid* did it!"

"What?" said Aunt Polly. She thought a moment. "Well, I'm sure you did some other mischief when I wasn't around!"

Tom knew his aunt was sorry she had hit him. But she would never admit it. He sat silent, feeling nothing but pity for himself. His eyes filled with tears as he pictured himself sick—maybe dying. Oh, wouldn't his aunt be sorry then!

Just then his cousin Mary came in, back from a visit in the country. She was all cheery and happy, and Tom just couldn't take it. As Mary brought her sunshine and joy in one door, Tom got up and took his clouds and gloom right out the other.

As he walked through the darkness, he got out his flower and thought about the new girl. Would she pity him? Would she put her arms around his neck and comfort him?

At the Thatcher house, he saw a candle lit in an upstairs window. Was *she* there? Tom climbed over the fence and moved under the window. He lay down. With his hands folded on his chest, he held the poor, wilted flower. This is how he would look when he died—all alone in the cold world. The girl would find him in the morning. And she would drop a tear upon his young, lifeless form. . . .

Suddenly, the window went up. Someone dumped a pan of water on the grass below. Tom was soaked! He jumped over the fence and shot home in the darkness.

As Tom got out of his wet clothes, Sid woke up. He could see the danger in Tom's eye and was wise enough to keep still.

The sun rose on a peaceful Sunday morning. Tom spent most of it trying to learn Bible verses for Sunday school. Sid, the goody-goody, had learned his lesson days before. Mary took Tom aside and tried her best to help him. She also shook out his Sunday suit and brushed his hair into curls, which he promptly smoothed out.

Then Mary, Tom, and Sid set off for Sunday school. The teachers there gave colorful tickets to children who learned their Bible lessons. By learning 2,000 verses, students could collect enough tickets to win their own Bibles.

Only a few older pupils had ever earned enough tickets to get a Bible. Mary got one after two years of hard work. Tom had little interest in the prize itself. But he longed for the glory and attention that came with it.

So on that bright Sunday morning, Tom planned to trade his treasures for tickets. He stood outside the church offering other children all the things he'd gotten from yesterday's whitewashing affair.

A church service was held right after Sunday school class. Most of the village was there. Judge and Mrs. Thatcher sat up front. Right beside them sat the beautiful new girl. When the Sunday school teacher asked if anyone had enough tickets for a Bible, Tom stepped forward. It was the surprise of the decade! The amazed teacher sensed a mystery here. Amy Lawrence looked proud and glad for Tom, but he wouldn't look at her.

Judge Thatcher was to award the prize. "Fine job, Thomas Sawyer," the Judge said. "Learning 2,000 verses is hard work. We are proud of boys who learn." Then he looked closely at Tom. "No doubt you know the names of the first two men who followed Jesus. Tell them to us, won't you?"

Tom tugged at a shirt button. He blushed and his eyes fell. At last he shouted out, "DAVID AND GOLIATH!"

It was a long time before the laughter ended. Finally, the gathering fell silent again.

The day was hot, and the sermon went on and on. Tom was really suffering! Then he thought of a treasure he still had in his pocket. It was a large black beetle, a "pinch-bug," he called it. But as soon as Tom took the bug out of a little box, it bit him on the finger! The hurt finger went into the boy's mouth, and the beetle flipped into the aisle.

An old poodle dog happened to be sitting in the corner. He spied the beetle and walked toward it. As he gave it a sniff, it bit him on the chin. Then there began a war of sorts between the poodle and the beetle. It ended with the poodle sitting on the bug and then yelping round and round the room!

By this time every person in church was redfaced and choking with laughter. Tom Sawyer felt quite cheerful as he walked home. The only bad part of the whole thing was that the dog had flattened his pinch-bug.

| 3 |
Heartbreak

On Monday morning Tom Sawyer was miserable, as usual. He was always unhappy on Mondays—the beginning of another week of suffering in school.

As Tom walked to school, he came upon Huckleberry Finn. Everybody in town knew that Huck's no-good father was always drinking. Huck didn't go to school or wear clean clothes. He used bad language and wasted his days away. All of the village mothers thought he was very, very bad. All of the boys thought he was a hero!

As usual, Huck was dressed in men's clothes that were way too big for him. A ragged old coat hung nearly to his heels. The cuffs of his baggy pants dragged in the dirt.

"Hello, Huckleberry!" shouted Tom. "What's that you got?"

"Dead cat."

"Say, what's a dead cat good for?"

"It's just the thing to make warts go away," said Huck.

"How's it work?" asked Tom.

"Well, you find a cat and take it to the graveyard along about midnight. When someone bad has been put there, the devils will come. You can't see them. You can only hear a sound like the wind. Then, when the devils take the bad fellow away, you heave your cat after them. You say, 'Devil follow corpse! Cat follow devil! Warts follow cat!' That will get rid of *any* wart."

"Did you ever try it, Huck?"

"No, but I'm going to try it tonight. Those devils are sure to come for that bad man they buried Saturday. They had to wait until tonight. You know they couldn't come on a Sunday!"

"Let me go with you, Huck! Come by my window tonight and meow for me."

Huck nodded. "Sure, Tom. I'll be there by the silver moon."

Walking on, Tom finally reached the little

schoolhouse. He slipped in the door quickly and hung his hat on a peg.

"You there—Thomas Sawyer!" called out the schoolmaster in a stern voice.

"Sir!"

"Why are you late—*again?*"

Tom was about to make up a story. Then he saw two yellow braids hanging down a lovely back. He also saw that the only empty spot in the girls' section was right beside the new girl. He had an idea.

"I STOPPED OFF TO HAVE A WORD WITH HUCKLEBERRY FINN," Tom called out loud and clear.

Everyone turned and stared.

"Thomas Sawyer," growled the schoolmaster, "you will go and sit with the *girls*! Let that be a lesson to you!"

Tom sat down on the pine bench. There were winks and whispers around the room. But by and by, no one noticed him anymore.

Tom began to write on his slate. For a while, the girl pretended not to notice. But then she became curious.

"Let me see it," she whispered.

Tom had drawn some little pictures—a horse, a man, and a girl coming along.

"That's ever so nice," the girl whispered. "I wish I could draw."

"I'll learn you," Tom whispered back, "—at noon. What's your name?"

"Becky Thatcher. What's yours? Oh, I know. It's Thomas Sawyer."

"Call me Tom, will you?"

Now Tom began to write something on the slate. He hid the words from the girl. But then he let her push his hand away until she could read the words, *"I love you."*

Becky Thatcher turned red. "Oh, you bad thing!" she said. But she looked pleased.

Just then, Tom felt someone grab at his ear. The schoolmaster angrily dragged him back to the boys' side of the room and pushed him down into his old seat. Tom tried to look sorry. But even though his ear hurt, his heart was happy.

At noon, Tom and Becky went into the schoolyard with the others. But after a moment they sneaked back into the empty schoolroom for Becky's drawing lesson.

"Say, Becky," Tom said shyly, "was you ever engaged?"

"What's that?" Becky asked.

"Why, engaged to be married. You just tell a boy you won't ever love anybody but him. And then you kiss. That's all." Then Tom leaned close to Becky's ear. "I love you," he whispered. "Now you whisper it to me—just the same!"

Becky bent shyly toward his ear and whispered, "I—love—you!"

Then she sprang away laughing and ran round and round the benches. Tom chased her. When he caught her he said, "Now, it's all done but the kiss."

Then he kissed her red lips. "Now it's all done, Becky. It will be ever so much fun. Why, me and Amy Lawrence—"

Becky's look stopped him.

"Oh, Tom! Then I ain't the *first* girl you've been engaged to?" She began to cry.

"Don't cry, Becky," said Tom. "I don't care for her no more." He tried to put his arm around her, but she pushed it away.

Tom got out his greatest treasure—a brass

knob that had come off the top of a fireplace tool. "*Please,* Becky, won't you take it?" he pleaded.

When she threw the knob to the floor, Tom marched out of the schoolhouse. After he'd gone, Becky ran to look after him.

"Tom! Come back, Tom!"

When there was no answer, she sat down to cry. Then the other students came in, and she had to hide her broken heart.

Far over the hills, Tom Sawyer sat alone in the woods. He felt sorry for himself. He thought that Becky had treated him like a dog! She would be sorry someday—maybe when it was too late! Maybe he would run away and become a pirate. Yes, that was it. It was settled. "It's Tom Sawyer, the pirate!" he said aloud. He would start right away!

| 4 |
Murder in the Graveyard

That night Tom lay in bed, listening for Huckleberry Finn. He must have dozed off, for he didn't hear the clock chime 11:00. Then a loud meow woke him. Tom checked to see that Sid was asleep. Then he dressed quickly and went out the window.

Huck was there with the dead cat in his hand. The boys moved off into the darkness. Within half an hour or so they were wading through the tall grass of the graveyard.

It was an old cemetery. Most of the tombstones were tipped over or broken. The wind moaned through the trees as if it were the spirits of the dead.

"Huck," Tom whispered, "do you think the dead people *like* for us to be here?"

Huck shook his head. "I wish I knowed."

Then Tom grabbed Huck's arm and whispered, "Look over there! What is it?"

Three figures came out of the gloom. One figure was swinging a lantern.

"It's the devils, sure enough!" whispered Huck. "Lordy, Tom, we better pray!"

"Now I lay me down to sleep . . ." Tom began to mumble.

"Shhh!" hissed Huck. "*Listen!* They're humans! I know old Muff Potter's voice."

Tom listened as hard as he could. "I know another one of them voices," he whispered. "It's mean ol' Injun Joe!"

The figures came closer. Now the boys could see the man who carried the lantern. It was young Dr. Robinson.

"What can they be up to?" Huck asked.

Old Muff Potter and Injun Joe had a wheelbarrow, a rope, and a couple of shovels. They started to dig up the man who'd been buried on Saturday! It was clear they intended to rob the grave.

Dr. Robinson sat down and leaned his back against a tree. He was so close the boys could have touched him.

"Hurry, men!" he said in a low voice. "The moon might come out at any moment."

For a time there was no noise but the sound of digging. Then sure enough, the moon drifted out from behind the clouds. It cast a pale light on the scene.

Finally, the grave was open. The body was pulled out of the coffin and tied in the wheelbarrow with the rope.

"We'll need more money to finish the job," Injun Joe said to Dr. Robinson.

"I've already paid you," said the doctor.

"You done more than that!" Injun Joe sounded angry now. "Five years ago I got sent to jail because of you. You said I was a no-good bum. I swore I'd get even with you!"

He had his fist in the doctor's face.

But the doctor struck out very quickly, knocking Injun Joe to the ground.

Muff Potter ran up. "Here now! Don't hit my partner!" He grabbed the doctor, and the two men struggled on the grass. But Potter was drunk, as usual. He could hardly fight. The doctor picked up a piece of a tombstone and knocked him out cold.

Injun Joe saw his chance. He snatched up Potter's knife and stabbed Dr. Robinson. The doctor fell across Potter, splashing him with blood! At the same moment, the clouds blotted out the moon. Terrified, Huck and Tom took their chance to run off.

It was not long before Muff Potter came to. He saw the dead doctor on the ground and believed that *he* had killed the man. Injun Joe let him think just that.

"I didn't know what I was doing!" Muff Potter cried. "You won't tell, will you, Joe?"

"I won't tell," Injun Joe promised. "Now quit your crying. You go off that way. I'll go this way."

Injun Joe watched Potter move away. "Chicken-heart!" he muttered. He glanced at Muff Potter's knife still lying on the ground. Then he, too, ran from the graveyard.

A minute later, the murdered man, the body in the wheelbarrow, and the open grave were alone. All was silent again.

Huck and Tom kept running until they came to an old shed outside of town. They burst through the door and fell to the floor.

"I'm scared, Huck. What do you reckon will come of all this?" panted Tom.

"We better keep still," said Huck. "That old Injun Joe is a devil. He would just as soon do away with us, too! Tom—we got to *swear* to keep mum!"

Tom found a piece of chalk in his pocket. He wrote on an old shingle: *"Huck Finn and Tom Sawyer swears they will keep mum about their secret. May they drop down dead in their tracks if they tell."*

Huckleberry admired Tom's writing. He took

a pin from his pocket. Each boy poked at a finger and signed their oath in blood.

The next day, things only got worse for Tom Sawyer. Sid had seen Tom sneak out the window! Of course he'd told Aunt Polly. She felt she had no choice but to whip Tom. Worse than that, the old lady had cried and told him how he'd broken her old heart. She said there just weren't no use in trying with him anymore.

Tom's heart was sorer than his body. The next day he moped off to school. There he found the brass knob lying on his desk. Becky Thatcher had returned it.

By noon, the tale of the murder in the graveyard was flying all around town. Muff Potter's knife had been found next to the body. Everyone was sure he had killed Dr. Robinson. The whole town drifted toward the graveyard. The schoolmaster even closed school. Tom really didn't want to return to that awful place, but he was too curious to stay away.

As he joined the crowd, Tom felt a pinch on his arm. It was Huck. Standing together, they listened to people talk.

"The poor young doctor!"

"Muff Potter will hang for this as soon as they catch him!"

Tom grabbed Huck's shoulder. He pointed. There in the crowd was Injun Joe.

Just then someone shouted. *"There's Muff Potter! Don't let him get away!"*

The sheriff grabbed Potter by the arm. The poor fellow burst into tears. "I didn't do it, friends!" he sobbed.

"Is that your knife?" The frowning sheriff pointed to the bloody knife on the ground.

Then Injun Joe began his lies. He said he'd seen the murder with his own eyes. He said that Muff Potter stabbed Dr. Robinson. After that, poor Muff Potter had nothing more to say. He had been too drunk to remember what had really happened.

All that week, Tom's fearful secret kept him up at night. Every few days he visited Muff Potter in the jailhouse. Every time, he took little presents along with him. It made Tom feel just a little better.

| 5 |
The Pirate Crew Sets Sail

One thought took Tom's mind off his secret worries about Muff Potter. Becky Thatcher had stopped coming to school! Tom soon found out that she was ill. What if she should die! Suddenly, Tom was no longer interested in war. He didn't even care about becoming a pirate.

At last Becky returned. When Tom saw her walk into the schoolyard, his heart gave a leap. The next instant he was busy showing off. He yelled, did handsprings, and stood on his head. But none of his tricks caught Becky's eye. Was it possible that she hadn't noticed him?

He moved closer and gave a loud war-whoop. He snatched a boy's cap and threw it up on the schoolhouse roof. Then he broke through a group of boys, tumbling them around in every direction. At last, he fell right under Becky's nose.

She turned away, with her nose in the air. Tom heard her say to another girl, "Some people are always showing off!"

Tom's cheeks burned. Crushed and heartbroken, he gathered himself up and sneaked off. It was right then he made up his mind. It was now clear that nobody loved him. Well, they would be sorry—all of them. Yep, when they saw they had driven him away, they would *beg* for his forgiveness.

He left school and ran far down Meadow Lane. In the distance he could hear the school bell tinkle. Now he cried to think he would never hear that sound again.

Just then he met his pal, Joe Harper. Joe looked miserable, too. He said his mother had whipped him for drinking some cream without asking. Well, Joe hoped she would be happy now that she would never have to see him again!

Joe's plan was to become a hermit and live in a cave. Tom said he thought it would be better to become a pirate. That way, they could live on their own island in the middle of the Mississippi. Nobody lived on Jackson's Island, so that was the place they should go. Joe soon agreed there were some mighty good points about being a pirate.

The boys hunted up Huckleberry Finn, and he joined in their plan right away. They decided to meet at the river about midnight. Then they would begin their lives as pirates.

At exactly midnight, Tom arrived at the riverbank. He had some boiled ham and other bits of food. It was starlight, and very still. The mighty river lay like an ocean at rest. Tom gave a low whistle. It was quickly answered with two whistles. From the darkness a voice called out, "Who goes there?"

"Tom Sawyer, the Black Avenger of the Spanish Main. Name your names."

"Huck Finn, the Red-Handed, and Joe Harper, the Terror of the Seas." The names had been Tom's idea. He had found them in his favorite books.

The Terror of the Seas had brought along a side of bacon. Finn, the Red-Handed, had stolen a frying pan.

The three pirates roamed the riverbank until they "captured" a small log raft. With Tom in command and Huck and Joe at the oars, they floated downstream.

As they passed the sleeping town, the Black Avenger stood with his arms folded. He "looked his last" upon the scene of his former joys and recent sorrows. How he wished that Becky could see him now!

The other pirates were looking their last too. They looked so long, in fact, that they almost drifted past Jackson's Island. But at 2:00 in the morning the raft landed, and the boys waded to shore.

The first thing they did was to light a fire and cook some of the bacon.

"This is the life for me," said Tom. "You don't have to go to school and wash your face and all that foolishness. You see, a pirate don't *have* to do anything!"

As the three became sleepy, their talk died out. Huck, the Red-Handed, fell right to sleep. But Tom, the Black Avenger, and the Joe, the Terror of the Seas, had a little trouble. They were bothered by the fact that they had stolen food and that maybe they had done wrong by running away. But at last each boy's conscience eased up. The pirates fell peacefully to sleep.

When Tom woke up in the morning, he wondered where he was. He sat up and rubbed his eyes. Then he remembered.

He woke up the other pirates, and they began a grand day. They splashed in the water and shouted. They threw in a line, caught a fish, and fried it with more of the bacon. Never before had fish tasted so good! They dozed in the shade for a while.

But then they heard a strange, loud sound in the distance.

"What is it?" asked Joe.

Tom shook his head.

"Ain't thunder," said Huck. "Come on, men. Let's go take a look."

They sprang to their feet and hurried to the shore. About a mile below the village, they saw a ferryboat. Every now and then a cannon fired from her deck.

"Somebody has *drowned*!" cried Tom.

"You must be right," Huck agreed. "They're shooting cannons to make the body come to the top."

Then Tom exclaimed, "I know who's drowned—it's *us*! They think we're dead!"

Suddenly they felt like heroes. They were missed. Hearts were breaking because of them. Tears were being shed. Say, wasn't this just *fine*? They were famous. It was worthwhile to be a pirate, after all.

When nightfall came, Huck and Joe went to sleep. Tom watched them for a while. But then he had an idea. He quietly got up and headed quickly for the riverbank.

The raft had drifted away, but that didn't stop him. He was able to wade halfway across the river. Then he swam the rest of the way. Walking through back alleys, he soon reached his aunt's house.

He looked in the window and saw a candle burning. There sat Aunt Polly, Sid, Mary, and Joe Harper's mother.

Tom pushed the door open a crack. He squeezed through on his knees.

"What makes the candle blow?" said Aunt Polly. "Why, for land's sake, the door's come open! Sid, go shut it."

Tom hid under a table just in time.

"As I was saying," said Aunt Polly, "Tom wasn't *really* a bad boy. He never meant no harm—and he was the best-hearted child that ever was!" She began to cry.

"It was the same with my Joe," said Mrs. Harper. Then her voice broke, and she, too, sobbed as if her heart would break.

Tom could hear Mary crying along. Before long he was sniffling himself. Bit by bit he learned that people thought the missing lads had gone off on a raft and drowned. This was Wednesday. If they were still missing by Sunday, all hope would be gone. On Sunday, a funeral would be held.

Uncomfortable as he was under the table, Tom had to keep still and listen. Then at last Mrs. Harper left, and the others went off to bed. Tom crept out of his hiding place. He tiptoed into Aunt Polly's room. She was moaning a little in her sleep. Tom thought about waking her up, but he didn't. Instead, he bent over and kissed her faded lips. Then he left, quietly latching the door behind him.

It was daylight when Tom got back to the island. He told Joe and Huck where he had been and what he had heard. They liked the idea of being missing heroes.

Tom was tired. He went to a shady spot to get some sleep. The other pirates got ready to fish and do some more exploring.

6

Pirates at Their Own Funeral

By Saturday afternoon, the boys' spirits were not so high. Joe Harper was homesick. He sat poking in the sand. Finally he said, "Oh, let's give it up. I want to go home. I want to see my mother." Without another word, he stood up and began wading toward the Illinois shore.

"I want to go too, Tom," said Huck. "This adventure don't seem so much fun anymore. And without Joe here, it'll be worse."

Huck moved toward the shore, too.

"Wait! *Wait!*" shouted Tom. "I want to tell you something."

Tom told the boys his secret plan. He had been thinking about it since the night he'd spied on Aunt Polly.

Joe and Huck agreed that it was a great idea.

He should have told them sooner! They would stay on the island after all. The lads went happily back to their games.

The mood in town was not so happy that Saturday. There was great grief and many tears. Becky Thatcher found herself moping around the empty schoolyard.

"Oh, if only I had kept his brass knob," she cried. "Now I haven't a single thing to remember him by."

The next morning the church bell tolled and the villagers gathered. No one could remember when the church had ever been so full. Aunt Polly came in, followed by Sid and Mary. Then the Harper family came in, all dressed in black.

The funeral began. The minister talked about the fine lost lads. Soon everyone in the church was weeping and wailing.

Then the church door creaked. The minister raised his streaming eyes and stared. First one person, then another, turned to look. The three dead boys came marching up the aisle—Tom in the lead, Joe next, and Huck in the rear. They had been hiding outside, listening to their own funeral!

Aunt Polly, Mary, and the Harpers threw themselves upon their loved ones. They showered Tom and Joe with kisses and hugs.

Huck stood off to one side of the aisle, looking uneasy.

"Aunt Polly, it just ain't fair," said Tom. "*Someone*'s got to be glad to see Huck!"

"Well, I'm right glad to see Huckleberry, poor motherless thing!" cried Aunt Polly. Then she hugged Huck too, making him squirm even more.

The congregation sang with all their hearts. Tom Sawyer the Pirate felt that this was the proudest moment of his life. That had been his secret plan—to return with his brother pirates and go to their own funeral.

The next day Tom and Joe were the heroes of the schoolyard. Before long the two pirates became quite stuck-up.

Tom decided he would ignore Becky Thatcher. He pretended he didn't see her. In turn, she began showing off. She ran and chased and screamed—always looking Tom's way to see if he noticed.

But instead of looking over at Becky, Tom began talking to Amy Lawrence.

That was too much for Becky. She moved to where Tom was sure to hear her. Then she began inviting the other boys and girls to a picnic. She invited everyone but Tom and Amy.

Tom tried to ignore this, too. But then he spied Becky sitting on a bench with Alfred Temple. That sight filled him with red-hot jealousy. "Any other boy," Tom thought, "but that Alfred Temple! He dresses so fine and thinks he's so smart. All the grownups think he's perfect!"

Tom went home at noon. He could stand it no more. When Becky saw that he was gone, she burst into tears.

"What's wrong?" asked Alfred.

"*Just go away, Alfred.* Leave me alone!" cried Becky. "I hate you!"

Alfred hurried back inside, angry and embarrassed. He guessed the truth and resolved to get even with Tom Sawyer. Inside the schoolhouse, he saw Tom's spelling book. Here was his chance. He opened the book and poured ink on the day's lesson.

Becky, looking in a window, saw what Alfred had done. She thought about Tom and Amy Lawrence. Yes, she *hated* him! She would just let him get in trouble!

At home, Aunt Polly went back and forth between being happy to see Tom and angry at him. "How could you do that to me? I was sick over you!" she cried.

Then Tom told her about the night he had visited. "I was going to tell you we'd gone pirating. But I got full of the idea of us coming to our own funeral. Now I wish that you'd waked up when I kissed you."

His aunt's eyes grew tender. "Why did you kiss me, Tom?"

"It made me sad that you was crying—because I love you!"

The old lady's voice shook. "You can kiss me now, Tom. Then be off with you!"

A moment later she stood watching him go. "I would forgive that boy a million times!" she cried.

7

Tom Takes Becky's Punishment

Aunt Polly's kiss lifted Tom's spirits. By the time he was back at school he was feeling happy again. His good mood made him take another chance with Becky. He went up to her and said, "I know I acted mighty mean to you, Becky—and I'm sorry. Please make up, won't you?"

"I'll thank you to keep to yourself, Mr. Tom Sawyer," Becky said bitterly. "I don't plan to ever speak to you again!"

She tossed her head and turned away. Tom was stunned. When he saw her again, he said something mean to her. She said something mean right back. So the war was on again. In fact, Becky could hardly wait to see Tom whipped for the ink in his spelling book.

Poor girl! She did not know how quickly she was nearing trouble herself.

The schoolmaster, Mr. Dobbins, had always wanted to be a doctor. He kept a mysterious book in his desk that told all about the human body. On this day, it happened that Becky was passing that desk when she saw the key in the lock. She looked around and saw that she was alone in the room.

The next instant, she had the book in her hands. She turned a page and saw a picture of a human figure. It was stark naked!

Just then, a shadow fell across the page. Tom Sawyer had stepped in the door. As he caught a look at the picture, Becky quickly closed the book. By accident, she tore the picture page right in half! She pushed the book back in the desk, turned the key, and burst out crying.

"Tom Sawyer, you *awful* boy! I just know you're going to tell on me. Now I'll be whipped! I never was whipped in school before."

Then she stamped her little foot and cried, "All right, be mean if you want to, then. You just wait and see!" And she rushed out of the schoolhouse.

"Shucks!" Tom Sawyer said to himself. "Never been licked in school! Ain't that just like a girl—they're so thin-skinned and chicken-hearted. Well, *of course* I ain't going to tell old Dobbins on her. But he'll see the look on her face, and he's going to know! Wouldn't she like to see me in just such a fix! Well, let her sweat it out!"

Then the students marched in, and school began. It wasn't long before the spelling book discovery was made. Becky almost stood up and told on Alfred Temple. But she didn't. "Tom will just tell on me about the picture," she told her herself, "so I won't say a word—not to save his life!"

After his whipping, Tom went back to his seat, not at all upset. He wondered if he'd spilled the ink without remembering it.

An hour went by. The warm air was drowsy with the hum of study. By and by, Mr. Dobbins unlocked his desk. He reached in for his book. Two of the pupils watched carefully as Dobbins settled back to read. Tom shot a glance at Becky. Once he had seen a hunted rabbit look just like she did now. That doomed look made him forget his quarrel with her. Something must be done!

But it was too late! The schoolmaster rose and faced the class.

"Who tore this book?" he asked angrily.

There was not a sound. You could have heard a pin drop.

"Benjamin Rogers, did you tear this book?"

"No, sir." Another pause.

"Joseph Harper, did you?"

Another no. Tom grew more uneasy as the master asked each boy, and then turned to the girls.

"Amy Lawrence?"

A shake of the head.

Dobbins went down the row. The girl in the next seat was Becky Thatcher. "Rebecca Thatcher?"

Her face was white with fear.

"Did you tear—now, look me in the face, Rebecca—did *you* tear this book?"

Tom sprang to his feet with a great leap. "I DONE IT!" he shouted out loudly.

Then he stepped forward to get his punishment. Out of Becky's eyes a look of thanks and love shone upon him. To Tom, that seemed pay enough for a *hundred* whippings! Without a whimper, Tom took the worst whipping Dobbins had ever given. He didn't even care that he had to stay two hours after school. He knew who would be waiting for him outside.

That night Tom went to bed with Becky's words ringing in his ears. "Tom," she had said, "how *could* you be so noble!"

8

Saving Muff Potter

Just before summer vacation, the schoolmaster held "Exam Night." At 8:00 in the evening the schoolhouse was brightly lit. Mr. Dobbins sat upon his chair with the blackboard behind him. His pupils and their parents sat before him. One by one the pupils said verses and answered questions.

The geography questions came near the end of the night. The schoolteacher turned his back on the group and drew a map on the board. Laughter began to ripple through the crowd.

A *cat* was slowly being lowered through an opening in the ceiling. It hung from a rope just over the teacher's head! Clawing at the air, the poor cat had a rag tied about its jaws to keep it from meowing. The laughter grew. Then one paw grabbed at the schoolmaster's head and snatched up his wig. The lights now gleamed off his bald head!

That broke up the meeting. Summer vacation had come.

Summer was slow. Becky Thatcher went on vacation, and it seemed to Tom that there was now no bright side to life.

Then came the measles. For two long weeks, Tom lay in bed. When he got back on his feet at last, he found that everyone in town had "got religion." Joe Harper was reading the Bible. Even Huck Finn was quoting verses. It sent Tom right back to his bed.

He was sick for three more weeks. When he got up this time, he drifted around until he found Joe and Huck in an alley. They were eating a stolen melon. Tom felt better now that his friends were themselves again.

Then the time came for Muff Potter's murder trial. The village talked of nothing else. Every word about the murder made Tom shiver. The night before the trial, Tom took Huck to a lonely place for a talk.

"Huck, have you ever told anybody about . . . *that*?"

"Of course I haven't! We wouldn't be alive two days if Injun Joe found out."

"Well," said Tom, "I reckon we're safe as long as we keep still. We better swear another oath of silence." And so they did.

Later, the two boys drifted toward the jail. They went to the cell window and called hello to Muff Potter.

"You've been good friends to me, boys," Muff called back. "Better than anybody else in this town. Boys, I guess I done an *awful* thing. I was drunk and crazy at the time, and now I got to hang for it."

That night, Tom's dreams were full of frights and horrors.

All the next day he hung about the courtroom. He felt drawn to go in, but forced himself to stay out. Huck was there too, feeling the same way.

Tom stayed out very late that night. There was something important he had to do.

Next day, Muff Potter was brought into court. The old man looked pale and tired and wore heavy chains.

Injun Joe was there, too.

Several people were called to the stand. They said they had seen Potter acting mighty guilty. Poor old Potter put his face in his hands and groaned.

Then it was time for Potter's lawyer to speak. He rose and turned to the clerk. "Call Thomas Sawyer to the stand!" he said.

Everyone looked surprised, including Muff Potter. Every eye watched as Tom took his place on the witness stand. The boy seemed mighty scared.

"Thomas Sawyer, where were you about midnight on June 17?"

Tom looked at Injun Joe. At first he could not speak. After a minute he whispered, "In the graveyard."

"A bit louder, please."

"In the graveyard! I was hid."

"Where? Were you near the grave where the murder happened?"

"I was behind the trees that's on the edge of the graveyard."

"Take your time, boy. Tell us everything that happened. Don't be afraid."

Tom began. At first he spoke slowly, but soon his words flowed easily. The room was silent except for his voice. "... and the doctor knocked down Muff Potter. Then Injun Joe jumped up with the knife and ..."

Crash! Quick as lightning, Injun Joe knocked over his chair, sprang for a window, and was gone!

Tom was a hero again. He was the pet of the old and the envy of the young. His name was in the village paper. There were some who believed Thomas Sawyer would be president some day!

The whole town was being good to Muff Potter now, too.

Tom's days were full of good times. But his nights were full of horror. He would not go out after dark, and Injun Joe was in every dream. By day, Tom was glad he had spoken up. At night he wished he'd have kept quiet.

Poor Huck was scared, too. Tom had gone to the lawyer's house that night and told the *whole* story. The lawyer had promised to keep Huck's name a secret. Still, Huck was sore afraid that his part might leak out. Tom had broken his oath of silence! Now Huck's faith in promises was gone.

Half the time, Tom worried that Injun Joe would never be caught. The other half, he was afraid that he *would* be. Either way, he felt sure he could never draw a safe breath until that man was dead.

Rewards had been offered, but Injun Joe was not found. The slow days drifted on. As each day passed, Tom felt a little safer.

| 9 |
The Buried Treasure

At one time or another, every boy gets an urge to go looking for treasure. One day, this urge came upon Tom Sawyer. On that same day, Tom happened upon Huck Finn, the Red-Handed. Huck was happy to go along.

"Where'll we dig?" asked Huck.

"It's best to look for treasures around old trees or under the floors of haunted houses. That's where robbers mostly bury them," Tom explained.

"Don't the robbers come back after their treasure, Tom?"

"No. They usually forget where they left it. Or else they die. Anyway, it lays there a long time. By and by somebody finds an old yellow paper that tells how to find it. I say we try digging up at the old haunted house on Still-House Hill."

Taking a pick and a shovel, they made the three-mile tramp to the haunted house.

"Say, Huck," said Tom, "what will you do with your share of treasure?"

"Well, I'll have pie and a glass of soda every day. And I'll go to every circus that comes along."

"Ain't you going to save any of it?"

"*Save* it? What for? Pa would just come back and get his claws on it. He'd clean it out quick enough! What are you going to do with yours, Tom?"

"I'm going to buy a new drum and a real sword. I'll get a red necktie and a puppy, too. And I'll get married."

"*Married!* Why, Tom Sawyer, you ain't in your right mind!" Then Huck thought a while. "If you get married, Tom, I'll be more lonesome than ever."

"No, you won't, Huck. You'll come and live with me. Now let's get to digging."

They dug under an old tree for half an hour, but they had no luck.

"Do they always bury it as deep as this?"

Huck asked, wiping sweat from his face.

"I reckon we haven't got the right spot." Tom thought hard. "I know! We got to come back at midnight. Then we look for the shadow of a dead tree. *That*'s the spot to dig!"

The boys were back that night. They looked for the shadow and began digging again. Their hole got deeper and deeper. At last Tom said, "It ain't no use, Huck. We're wrong again. Let's try looking inside the haunted house."

Huck shook his head. "I don't much like haunted houses," he said. "I couldn't bear to see a ghost."

"Ah, shucks! You know ghosts don't travel around but only at night. If we dig in the day they won't bother us."

So Huck and Tom left their pick and shovel behind and went home for the night.

About noon the next day, they were back. They dug a little at their last hole. Then they carried their tools up to the haunted house.

It felt mighty lonely there. They crept to the door and peeped inside. They saw a room with a dirt floor, an old fireplace, and broken windows. Cobwebs hung everywhere. The boys entered softly, talking in whispers. Their pulses beat fast. Their muscles were tense and ready to run.

After looking around below, they climbed the old stairs. They found nothing and were about to go down when . . .

"Shhh!" said Tom.

"What is it?" whispered Huck. His face was white with fright.

"*Shhh!* Hear it?"

"Yep! Let's run!"

"Keep still! Don't move! They're coming right toward the door!"

The boys lay flat. They peeked through a hole in the floor.

"There they are, Huck! Don't say another word. Oh, I wish I was out of this!"

Two men came in. The boys had seen one of them before. He was the old deaf and dumb fellow who'd been hanging around lately. He dressed like a Spaniard in a big wide-brimmed hat. A blanket with bright stripes covered his shoulders. Long white hair flowed from under the hat. Bushy white whiskers and green colored glasses hid his face. The other man was a total stranger.

"I don't like any of this one bit," the stranger said. "It's dangerous."

To the boy's amazement, the "deaf and dumb" Spaniard answered. "Dangerous?" he grunted. "You *coward*!"

The boys gasped. It was Injun Joe's voice! Shaking and silent, they watched as the men ate bread from their pocket.

"I'm dead for sleep!" yawned Injun Joe. Before long, both men were snoring.

"Now's our chance, Huck!" Tom urged. "Come on!"

But before they could leave, Injun Joe sat up. He woke his partner. "Time for us to move on," he said. "What will we do with the money that's left?"

"We could leave it here like before. No use taking it away until we go south for good. Six hundred in silver is a lot to carry."

The boys forgot their fears for the moment. What luck! Six hundred dollars was money enough to make half a dozen boys rich!

Injun Joe was on his knees now, digging in the dirt floor. He was about to bury the money when his knife struck something.

"What's this?" he said.

He drew out an old tin box. "Look, man, it's *money*!" he cried. The box was full of gold coins. "Partner, there must be thousands of dollars here!"

"What are we going to do with it—leave it here?" asked Joe's partner.

"No," said Injun Joe. "Look at that shovel over there. I just noticed that it has fresh dirt on it. Somebody's been around here."

Huck and Tom looked at each other. They'd forgotten their pick and shovel!

"We'll take the loot to my den. I'll bury it under the cross," said Injun Joe.

"Then we can get out of here right now," the other man said.

"Not yet," said Injun Joe. "Not until I've finished my work. I still have to get my revenge!"

It was twilight by the time the men left the house. They headed toward the river with their box full of coins.

Tom and Huck got up. Did they follow the two men? Not they! They were happy just to be alive! They walked home, hating themselves and their bad luck. Why had they left the shovel there? If not for that, Injun Joe would have hidden the gold and gone away. They would have been rich!

The boys decided to keep a watch for that Spaniard. They would follow him to his den, wherever that might be.

Then a terrible thought came into Tom's head. "*Revenge!* Injun Joe said he was going to get revenge! What if he meant *us,* Huck?"

10

Tom and Becky in the Cave

The next morning Tom heard good news. Judge Thatcher's family had come back to town. With Becky's return, Injun Joe and the treasure went to the back of Tom's mind.

Becky talked her mother into letting her have a picnic. Some of the younger Sunday school teachers were put in charge of the children. A ferryboat was chartered, and baskets were packed. Sid was sick and had to miss the fun. Mary stayed home with him. The rest of the happy group set off.

The last thing Mrs. Thatcher said to Becky was, "You'll be gone late. Perhaps you'd better stay all night with Susy Harper. Her family lives near the ferry landing."

The ferryboat carried the party down the river.

It tied up near a wooded hollow below town. Everyone dashed ashore with much shouting and laughter. The children played in the sun, had a fine picnic lunch, and then rested in the shade.

Then someone called out, "Who's ready to explore the cave?"

Everybody was! Bundles of candles were pulled out and everyone ran up the hill. The mouth of McDougal's cave was shaped like the letter *A*. Its big oak door stood open.

The cave itself was a network of crooked tunnels. They ran into each other and out again and led nowhere. No man really knew his way around the tunnels. It was an impossible thing. But Tom Sawyer knew as much of the cave as anyone.

The group of children moved down the main tunnel for nearly a mile. By and by, they went back to the mouth of the cave, happy with their grand day. They were surprised to find that so much time had gone by. Night was at hand, and the clanging bell of the ferry called to them.

On Sunday, the next day, Mrs. Thatcher saw Mrs. Harper at church. "Is my Becky still sleeping?" Mrs. Thatcher asked. "I suppose she is very tired from the picnic."

"Your Becky?" Mrs. Harper asked in surprise.

"Why, yes. Didn't she stay at your house last night?"

"No, I haven't seen her."

Mrs. Thatcher turned pale.

Just then Aunt Polly passed by. "Good morning, Mrs. Thatcher. Say, Mrs. Harper, I've got a boy that seems to be missing. I reckon my Tom must have stayed at your house last night. Now he's probably afraid to come to church."

"Oh, dear! He didn't stay with us," Mrs. Harper replied. She turned to her son. "Joe, when did you see Tom last?"

Joe tried to remember, but he was not sure. People began to whisper. Children were questioned. The young teachers were questioned. No one could remember seeing Tom and Becky on the ferry trip home. Then one young man said he feared they were still in the cave! At that, Mrs. Thatcher fainted. Aunt Polly fell to crying.

All that day, the town seemed empty and

dead. The women sat with Aunt Polly and Mrs. Thatcher. The men went to the cave. All night long the town waited for news.

The next morning a message came: "Send more candles and food." The search for the missing children went on.

Now, to return to Tom and Becky in the cave...

The two had tripped along the tunnels with the rest of the group. Then they had wandered off alone. They held their candles high and read the names that people had scratched on the cave walls.

Drifting along and talking, they didn't notice that they had moved into a strange part of the cave. Here there were no names on the walls. Winding this way and that, they finally scrambled down a stairway of cave rock. They were in a huge rock room! Thousands of bats were bunched under its roof. The candlelight seemed to bother these creatures, because they started to squeak and dart about. One bat struck Becky's candle with its wing. Its flame went out.

Tom hurried her to another part of the cave.

There they found a little underground lake. Now, for the first time, the children noticed the gloomy quiet of the place.

"It seems ever so long since I heard the other children," Becky said. "We better start back, Tom."

"Yes, I reckon we better."

"Can you find the way, Tom?"

Tom didn't answer. They started through one tunnel. But it all looked strange.

Tom yelled out for help. But the echo of his own voice was the only answer.

"Tom! We're lost!" Becky cried. "We will *never* get out of this awful place! Oh, why did we leave the others?"

She sank to the ground crying. Tom put his arms around her.

Then they moved on again. By and by Tom blew out their second candle. Becky understood that they needed to save it.

Finally poor Becky grew so tired she could go no farther. They shared a piece of cake from Tom's pocket. Then they slept.

Tom woke first. He knew he must *do* something, so he decided to explore the tunnels alone. He took a kite string from his pocket and tied it to a rock. Then he walked away, unwinding the string as he went.

Suddenly, Tom saw something in the darkness. A candle came around the corner. It was held by a human hand!

Tom shouted for joy. Then, instantly, that hand was followed by the body it belonged to. *It was Injun Joe!* Tom stood frozen with fear. Luckily, the shout had scared Injun Joe. He turned and ran, quickly disappearing into the darkness. Tom was so weak with fright that he could barely make it back to Becky. Wisely, he did not tell her about seeing Injun Joe. The poor girl was frightened enough.

By the next day, Becky was weaker and losing hope. She said she would wait—where she was—and die.

Back at the town, the villagers mourned. The children had not been found, and most people thought they were done for. Mrs. Thatcher had become very ill, and Aunt Polly's gray hair had turned almost all white.

Then, in the middle of the night, the village bells began to ring out. In a moment the streets were full of people. "Turn out! Turn out!" they shouted. "The children are found! They're *found*!"

Every light was lit. It was the happiest night the little town had ever seen.

Soon Tom lay upon a sofa telling his story. He told how three times he had gone searching as far as his string would let him. On the third trip, he'd seen a tiny light up ahead. It was a hole to the outside! He'd rushed back to get Becky. Together, they had climbed out of the hole in the cave.

After crying for joy, they had made their way to the river. Before long a boat had picked them up *five miles* from the mouth of the cave!

Tom and Becky were so tired that they rested for two weeks. When Tom got up, he set right off to see Huck. On his way down to the river, he stopped by Judge Thatcher's house to visit Becky.

"Well, Thomas," Judge Thatcher said, "nobody will get lost in that cave again."

"Why?" Tom asked.

"Because I had an iron lock put on that big door two weeks ago."

Tom turned as white as a sheet.

"What's the matter, boy? Someone bring this child a glass of water!"

The water was brought and thrown in Tom's face.

"Now you're all right. Whatever was the matter with you, Tom?"

"Oh, Judge—Injun Joe's in the cave!"

11
Floods of Gold

The news of Injun Joe being trapped in the cave spread quickly. A group of men boarded boats and set off to McDougal's cave. Tom Sawyer made sure to ride in the boat that carried Judge Thatcher.

When the cave door was unlocked, everyone saw an awful sight. Injun Joe lay stretched upon the ground. He was dead. That made Tom feel sad. He had been lost in that cave himself. He knew how Injun Joe had suffered. Yet now he also felt safe. It was as if a great weight of fear had been lifted from him.

The next day, Tom took Huck to a quiet place to talk. "Huck, I think Injun Joe hid all that money in the cave!"

Huck's eyes blazed. "Aw, shucks! Do you mean it, Tom?"

"I'm telling the truth, Huck, if ever I was. Will you go in there with me to get it out?"

"You bet I will! Can we find it without getting lost?"

"Huck, we can do that without the least bit of trouble. Just wait until we get there! If we don't find the money, I'll give you my drum and everything I've got in the world."

"Let's start right off, Tom."

The boys got together some supplies. They gathered bread and meat, matches and candles, and two or three kite strings. They borrowed a small boat from someone who happened to not be around.

Tom took Huck to the hole that led into the tunnels. "Won't this be the perfect hideout for our robber gang, Huck?" Tom asked. "And of course we won't tell anyone but Joe Harper and Ben Rogers."

The boys entered the hole, with Tom in the lead. They tied their kite strings fast, and moved carefully down the tunnel. Now they were whispering, for the gloom of the place had lowered their spirits.

"I'll show you something, Huck." Tom

lifted his candle high. "Look at the big rock over yonder. Do you see what's on it?"

"Why, it's a *cross!* Didn't Injun Joe say he'd bury the treasure under a cross?"

"Yes, he did. And that's right where I saw him, Huck!"

"Tom, let's get out of here!"

"What! And leave the treasure?"

"Yes! *Leave it!* Injun Joe's ghost is around here for sure."

"No it ain't, Huck. He died at the mouth of the cave—five miles from here."

That seemed to make Huck feel better. The boys searched around the rock for a while. Then Tom got an idea.

"He said *under the cross*, Huck. I'll bet the money is right under this rock." Tom began to dig and scratch in the clay. He had not dug four inches before he struck wood.

"Hey, Huck! Do you hear that?"

Then Huck began to dig, too. Sure enough, there was the treasure box.

"Got it!" said Huck. Opening the lid, he let the gold coins run through his fingers. "My, but we're rich, Tom!"

"Huck, I always reckoned we'd get it. But this is just too good to believe!"

The boys tried to lift the heavy box. They could move it a bit but not carry it.

"Good thing I brought these big old feed bags along," said Tom.

They put the money in the bags. Then they carried them to the boat and rowed to town.

Back on shore, Tom turned to Huck. "You wait here and watch the bags. I'll go and find us a wagon."

When Tom returned, they loaded the sacks into the wagon and threw some old rags on top. Then they started off toward the village, dragging their cargo behind them.

They hadn't gone far when they met Judge Thatcher. "Hello, boys!" he called. "Are you going to the party up at Widow Douglas's? What are you hauling? Come on along. Just bring your load with you."

Huck and Tom found themselves being led up the hill.

The Widow Douglas's place was grandly lighted. It seemed that *everybody* in the village was invited. The rest of the Thatchers were there. So were the Harpers and Aunt Polly, Sid, Mary, the minister, and a great many more. All were dressed in their best finery. Leaving the wagon near the door, Huck and Tom went in. The widow welcomed them as kindly as anyone could welcome two boys who were covered with dirt and smoky candle wax. Aunt Polly frowned at Tom.

Widow Douglas took the boys upstairs to wash up. Then everyone sat down to a fine supper. Even though the Widow Douglas often had parties, this one was special.

"The widow's got a secret she's going to tell tonight," Sid whispered.

Widow Douglas had been worried about poor Huck. She was thinking how he didn't have anybody and neither did she. Now she announced that she wanted to give Huckleberry Finn a home. She would send him to school. She would even start him up in business when she had enough money.

Tom broke in. "But Huck don't need it! Huck's *rich*! I reckon I can show you. Wait here a minute." He ran out and came back, struggling with the heavy sacks. He poured a flood of yellow coins upon the table. "There! What did I tell you? Half of it's Huck's, and half of it's mine!"

No one stirred as Tom told his tale.

Then the money was counted. The sum came to a little more than 12,000 dollars! It was more money than anyone there had ever seen at one time before.

The whole town soon knew the story. Every "haunted" house for miles was torn apart as people searched for treasure. And most of these treasure-hunters were grown men, not boys.

Wherever Tom and Huck went, people stared at them. Their story was printed in the newspaper. Judge Thatcher decided that Tom was a grand young lad. Some day he might become a great lawyer or soldier!

The Widow Douglas helped Huck put his money in the bank. Judge Thatcher did the same for Tom. Each lad now had a fine income—*a dollar every day*. That was a lot of money! Why, a grown person could live for a whole week on a dollar and a quarter.

Widow Douglas made sure that Huck was clean and neat, combed and brushed. He learned to eat with a knife and fork and to talk proper. In other words, the chains of society bound him hand and foot.

Huck bravely bore this misery for three weeks. Then he turned up missing. Tom found him hiding in an old shack. Huck was a happy mess—uncombed and wearing his ragged old clothes again. Tom told him how worried Widow Douglas was. He said that Huck should go back to her.

"I can't, Tom. It ain't for me. The widow is good to me, but I ain't used to her ways. I got to go to school and wear shoes all Sunday! *I can't stand it, Tom!* I wouldn't be in this mess if it weren't for all that money. You take my share—I don't want it!"

"I just can't do that, Huck," said Tom. Then he had an idea. "You know, Huck," Tom said seriously, "I can't let just *anybody* be in my robber gang. A fellow's got to be respectable."

"You wouldn't shut me out, would you, Tom?" cried Huck.

"I don't know, Huck. What would people say? I can't have no low characters giving my robber gang a bad name, you know."

Huck thought for a while. Then he said, "Well, I'll go back to the widow for a month. If you'll let me be in the gang, I'll try to stand it as best I can."

"All right, Huck! Come along, old chap. And I'll tell you what—I'll ask the widow to go easy on you for a while."

The boys started to walk toward Widow Douglas's house. "When are we going to start the gang and try out being robbers, Tom?" asked Huck.

"Oh, right off! We'll get the boys together tonight. We'll swear to stand by one another and kill anybody that hurts one of the gang."

"That's fine! That's *mighty* fine, Tom!"

"But the swearing has got to be done at midnight—in a lonesome, awful place. You know, a haunted house is best. But they're all ripped up now."

"This will be even more fun than pirating," cried Huck. "Why, I'll stay with the widow *forever* if I get to be a real robber! I'll make her proud she took me in!"

Afterword

So ends this story. It is the story of a *boy*, and so it must stop here. If it went much farther, it would become the story of a *man*.

Most of the characters from this book went on to live well and happily. Someday it may be a good idea to continue the story of the younger ones. Then we can see what sort of men and women they turned out to be.

Activities
The Adventures of Tom Sawyer

BOOK SEQUENCE
Number the events to show which happened first, second, and so on.

_____ 1. The Terror of the Seas brings along a side of bacon.

_____ 2. Tom tries to look unwilling as he hands Ben the brush.

_____ 3. In court, Tom breaks his oath of silence.

_____ 4. Tom plays hooky so he can go swimming.

_____ 5. Becky says she was never whipped in school before.

_____ 6. At last, Tom and Becky climb out of the cave.

_____ 7. The blue-eyed girl wears a white summer dress.

_____ 8. Huck tells Tom to take his share of the money.

_____ 9. On Sunday morning, Tom tries to learn Bible verses.

_____ 10. Tom hears that the funeral will be held on Sunday.

_____ 11. Joe and Tom fight an important army battle.

_____ 12. The boys peek through a hole in the floor.

_____ 13. Tom takes Muff some little presents at the jailhouse.

_____ 14. Tom is sorry the dog flattened his pinch-bug.

THE ADVENTURES OF TOM SAWYER | ACTIVITIES

CHARACTER STUDY
Reread Chapter 1 and answer below.

A. Circle two words that describe each character.

1. **Tom Sawyer** listless   disobedient
   abnormal   mischievous

2. **Aunt Polly** dutiful   savage
   suspicious   coldhearted

3. **Sid** boisterous   tattletale
   prissy   magnificent

4. **Ben Rogers** cheerful   sinister
   brilliant   gullible

5. **Becky Thatcher** warm-hearted   jealous
   inattentive   wicked

6. **Huckleberry Finn** gloomy   optimistic
   cunning   light-hearted

B. Use character names from the box to complete each sentence. You may use a name more than once.

Tom Sawyer   Aunt Polly   Sid   Ben Rogers

1. _____ said, "I'll lick you for that!"

2. _____ said, "Look, that thread is black."

3. _____ said, "I'll give you my apple if you'll let me."

4. _____ said, "They say that old fools is the biggest fools!"

5. _____ said, "What do you call work?"

81

THE ADVENTURES OF TOM SAWYER

6. _____ said, "Don't you wish you could go swimming?"

7. _____ said, "I'm afraid I've spoiled him."

TRUE OR FALSE
Write **T** or **F** to show whether each statement below is *true* or *false*.

1. ___ Aunt Polly was always afraid that she had spoiled Tom Sawyer.

2. ___ Sid broke a sugar bowl but Tom got blamed for it.

3. ___ Becky Thatcher did not mind that Tom had previously been engaged to Lawrence.

4. ___ Muff Potter was fooled into thinking that he killed Dr. Robinson.

5. ___ Along with Huckleberry Finn and Joe Harper, Tom ran away from home to look for the pirate's treasure on Jackson's Island.

6. ___ Since Tom, Huck and Joe attended their own funeral, they were treated like heroes.

7. ___ When Mr. Dobbins discovered the torn page which happened to be a picture of a naked body he angrily questioned Tom directly.

8. ___ At Muff Potter's murder trial, Tom was unable to tell the truth because he was afraid of Injun Joe's revenge.

9. ___ When Tom and Huck went treasure hunting in an old haunted house, they saw that Injun Joe found a buried box of gold coins.

THE ADVENTURES OF TOM SAWYER | ACTIVITIES

10. ___ Huck gave Tom all of his gold coins and never went back to Widow Douglas.

CAUSE AND EFFECT
Reread Chapter 4 and answer below.

A. Read the list of *causes* on the left. Then write a letter to match each *cause* with its *effect* on the right.

CAUSE

1. ___ Tom dozes off.
2. ___ The moon drifts out from behind the clouds.
3. ___ The doctor strikes out quickly.
4. ___ Muff Potter is so drunk that he can hardly fight.
5. ___ The sheriff points to Muff Potter's bloody knife.

EFFECT

a. He doesn't hear the clock chime 11.
b. The cemetery is lit with pale light.
c. Injun Joe falls to the ground.
d. Muff is locked up in the jailhouse.
e. The doctor knocks him out with a piece of tombstone.

B. Write **T** if the statement is *true* or **F** if the statement is *false*.

1. ___ The loud meow sound caused Tom to wake up.
2. ___ Opening the grave was the effect of digging.
3. ___ Injun Joe's anger was the cause of his feeling cheated.

THE ADVENTURES OF TOM SAWYER

4. ___ Tom and Huck ran off as an effect of witnessing a murder.

5. ___ Tom's sadness was the effect of finding the brass knob on his desk.

INFERENCE
Reread Chapter 10 and circle a letter to show the implied meaning of the **boldfaced** words.

1. With Becky's return, thoughts of Injun Joe and the treasure **went to the back of Tom's mind.**
    a. He lost his memory of what had happened.
    b. He could think of nothing but Becky.
    c. He was too frightened to think about it.
    d. He was no longer afraid of Injun Joe.

2. Becky **talked her mother into** letting her have a picnic.
    a. talked much faster than her mother did
    b. used big words her mother didn't understand
    c. begged and pleaded until her mother agreed
    d. sweetly asked her father to convince her mother

3. **Night was at hand**, and the clanging bell of the ferry called out to the children.
    a. It was beginning to get dark outside.
    b. Their hands were getting cold.
    c. It was now approaching midnight.
    d. The ferry was on hand to take them home.

THE ADVENTURES OF TOM SAWYER | ACTIVITIES

4. "Tom must have stayed at your house last night. Now he's probably **afraid to come to church**."
    a. frightened of the minister
    b. too dirty to show up at church
    c. nervous about facing Aunt Polly
    d. too tired to get up so early

5. The message from the searchers said, **"Send more candles and food."**
    a. The missing children had been found.
    b. The men from town had given up the search.
    c. The children were setting up a campsite.
    d. The children had not yet been found.

FINAL EXAM
Circle a letter to correctly answer each question or complete each sentence.

1. How did the book's author define "work"?
    a. tasks he wasn't paid to do
    b. any activity that made him sweat
    c. anything he didn't want to do
    d. anything that wasn't his own idea

2. Who did Tom Sawyer say were "the first two men to follow Jesus?"
    a. Peter and Paul
    b. David and Goliath
    c. Matthew and Mark
    d. Mary and Joseph

3. Three characters in the book who plotted to "get even" were
   a. Tom Sawyer, Alfred Temple, and Injun Joe.
   b. Becky Thatcher, Ben Rogers, and Injun Joe.
   c. Tom Sawyer, Huckleberry Finn, and Muff Potter
   d. Tom Sawyer, Amy Lawrence, and Huckleberry Finn.

4. Which two students watched with special interest as the schoolmaster opened his book?
   a. Becky and Amy
   b. Alfred and Sid
   c. Tom and Huck
   d. Tom and Becky

5. To keep track of the path he followed through the tunnels, Tom
   a. dropped breadcrumbs.
   b. scratched a line on the dirt floor.
   c. unrolled a kite string.
   d. made a map on a shingle.

6. Tom and Huck didn't recognize Injun Joe when they first saw him in the haunted house because
   a. he now looked older and thinner.
   b. he wore a disguise.
   c. he talked in a strange false voice.
   d. he hid his face.

Answers to Activities
The Adventures of Tom Sawyer

BOOK SEQUENCE
1. 8 2. 2 3. 11 4. 1 5. 10 6. 13 7. 4 8. 14
9. 5 10. 9 11. 3 12. 12 13. 7 14. 6

CHARACTER STUDY
A. 1. disobedient, mischievous
2. dutiful, suspicious
3. tattletale, prissy
4. cheerful, gullible
5. warm hearted, jealous
6. optimistic, light-hearted

B. 1. Tom Sawyer 2. Sid 3. Ben Rogers
4. Aunt Polly 5. Tom Sawyer
6. Ben Rogers 7. Aunt Polly

TRUE OR FALSE
1. T 2. T 3. F 4. T 5. T
6. T 7. F 8. F 9. T 10. F

CAUSE AND EFFECT
A. 1. a 2. b 3. c 4. e 5. d
B. 1. T 2. T 3. F 4. T 5. T

INFERENCE
1. b 2. c 3. a 4. c 5. d

FINAL EXAM
1. c 2. b 3. a 4. d 5. c 6. b